For Stella, my brave star,

who shines so bright

With special thanks to expert consultant

Kirsten Cullen Sharma, PsyD,

former director of the

Early Childhood Clinical Service,

NYU Child Study Center

The Fix-It Friends
Have No Fear!

Nicole C. Kear
illustrated by Tracy Dockray

[Imprint]
MAKE YOUR MARK

NEW YORK

[Imprint]
MAKE YOUR MARK

A part of Macmillan Publishing Group, LLC
175 Fifth Avenue, New York, NY 10010

Library of Congress Cataloging-in-Publication Data is available.

Our books may be purchased in bulk for promotional,
educational, or business use. Please contact your local
bookseller or the Macmillan Corporate and Premium Sales
Department at (800) 221-7945 ext. 5442 or by e-mail at
MacmillanSpecialMarkets@macmillan.com.

Book design by Ellen Duda
Illustrations by Tracy Dockray
Imprint logo designed by Amanda Spielman

First Edition—2017

ISBN 978-1-250-11577-5 (hardcover)

1 3 5 7 9 10 8 6 4 2

ISBN 978-1-250-08584-9 (paperback)

1 3 5 7 9 10 8 6 4 2

ISBN 978-1-250-08585-6 (ebook)

mackids.com

You know what I hate more than broccoli casserole and
missing recess and know-it-all brothers? Book thieves!

They are a big problem. Humongous.

Of course I know just how to fix them. Want to find out how I do it?

Just *try* to steal this book. Go ahead! Just you try and you
will regret it . . . or my name isn't Veronica L. Conti!

Chapter 1

My name's Veronica Conti and I'm seven. That means I've had seven whole years to learn things. Here's what I've figured out so far:

1. Everything tastes better when you put whipped cream on it. Even peas. Even—blegh! ugh! mercy!—broccoli.

2. When your big brother is acting super annoying, just pretend that a UFO is about to touch down any second and steal him. It makes you feel a lot better.

3. Everyone has problems.

The Fix-It Friends

Even worms have problems. I learned that when I tried to give my pet worm, Walter, a suntan. I left him on a big rock for a few hours, and when I came back, he was as dead as a doornail.

Grown-ups think kids don't have problems. They think just because you're a kid, your life is easy-peasy, all butterflies and rainbows and whipped cream for breakfast, lunch, and dinner. Ha!

I have a whole bunch of problems:

1. My big brother, Jude, who is nine.

2. Homework.

3. My dad's allergic to dogs, so I can't have one even though I really, really, really, really, really, really, really, really, really, *really* want one.

4. Did I mention Jude?

Thankfully, I'm pretty great at solving problems. Which is why I decided to start the Fix-It Friends. Maya was my first client. In fact, Maya was sort of the whole reason I started the group to begin with.

I met Maya on the first day of second grade. At recess, which is my favorite part of school. The rest of school can be pretty boring.

"It can't be all boring!" my mom always says, as cheery and bright as a big yellow sunflower.

"Oh yes, it can."

"What about writing workshop?"

"Writing makes my hand hurt."

"Or reading?"

"Reading too much gives me a headache."

"Or math?"

"Are you kidding?" I say. "I'd rather eat a bathtub full of broccoli than do subtraction."

"Broccoli is very high in calcium," my mom says.

"Not the point, Mom," I remind her.

"What about recess?"

She's got me there. Recess is the super-supreme best. It's when I get to see all my friends and turn cartwheels and jump rope and play tag, which is my all-time favorite! These are the people I play tag with almost every day:

1. Cora, who is my best friend. She has naturally curly hair, which is red, and freckles on her cheeks. If she were a dog, she would be a poodle. Sometimes I get jealous of her because I have always wanted red hair and curly hair and freckles and

she has all three, which kind of isn't fair. She says she is sometimes jealous of my hair, which is straight and blond, but I think she is just being polite. Cora is *always* polite. She loves school, even the most boring parts like practicing penmanship.

2. Camille, who is Cora's twin sister. They're identical. The really weird thing is that they have two five-year-old brothers named Bo and Lou who are twins, too! I am not even kidding. Camille has curly red hair just like Cora's, but her hair is always cut short, and it's a lot messier. Sometimes I find bits of twigs and leaves in her hair, and once there

was even a big acorn in there! Camille is a whiz with balls, especially basketballs. She can spin one on her fingertip like a pro! If she were a dog, I think she'd be a cocker spaniel.

3. Minerva, who everyone calls Minnie for short. Her grandma is from Puerto Rico, so she taught Minnie how to speak Spanish, and Minnie can say absolutely anything. She has taught me how to say important stuff in Spanish, like *"No brócoli para mí, gracias. Si me lo como, yo podría morir,"* which means "No broccoli for me, thanks. If I eat it, I could die." Minnie can play the piano with

both hands at the same time. In fact, she is so good at the piano that she can sometimes play without even looking at her hands! She has silky black hair, which she wears in two braids, and she is very tall and skinny, just like a greyhound.

4. Noah, who is the shortest boy in the second grade and also the fastest runner. He reminds me of a beagle because of his enormous brown eyes and floppy brown hair. Noah is the quiet type, which is my favorite type for a boy to be. He is kind of mysterious, but I do know a few things about him. He absolutely hates when people talk about

him being short, and he absolutely loves playing soccer. He wears a soccer jersey to school every single day. I think it's because of his dad, who used to be a famous soccer star in Brazil. Now his dad has his own sports show named after him called *The Rafael Rocha Radio Hour*, so I think he is still kind of famous . . . or his voice is, anyway.

So that's my tag group, and we have been playing together since first grade. Sometimes other kids join our tag game, and sometimes Jude comes over with his best friend, Ezra, and they teach us new kinds of tag like Air Tag and Backwards Tag and Dog Tag. Whenever we play Dog Tag, I'm a golden retriever because if I were a dog, that's the breed I would be. Guess what kind Jude pretends to be? None! He is always the dogcatcher.

Usually, though, it's just the five of us who play. Except if one of us is sick or injured. If you are really sick or injured, you go to the nurse, but if you are just a bit hurt, you sit with your lunch box by the fence.

I feel so sorry for the people who have to do that. It happened to me once, when I knocked my head into Camille's head and we both had to spend the rest of recess sitting by the fence. It was pure torture, I tell you!

So there I was, on the first day of second grade, at recess with the tag group. Except Minerva was missing.

"Hey, where's Minnie?" I asked.

"She has a headache, so Miss Tibbs told her to sit by the fence," squeaked Cora.

Cora has a super-squeaky voice. I can imitate her voice, and it always cracks her up. She sort of sounds like she's a mouse trapped in a girl's body. What makes it extra funny is that Camille's voice is real low and raspy, like a crocodile's.

"Minnie is by the fence?" I asked.

Cora nodded.

I gasped. Gasping is my favorite sound effect. It makes people sit up and pay attention.

"Then what are we WAITING FOR?" I shouted. "Our friend needs us!!"

I dashed over to the fence. Sure enough, there was Minnie. Her hair was in two neat braids as usual, and she was wearing a beautiful red headband, too. Minnie looked tired. She was leaning her chin on her hand.

"HERE I AM, MINNIE!!" I shouted.

She winced.

"Oh NO!" I yelled. "What can I DO?"

"Well, maybe you could talk a little more quietly?" she asked with a smile.

"Oh yes, of course!" I whispered. "Hey, maybe you have a headache from that headband. It might be pinching your brain." I love headbands, but I can never wear them for more than two minutes because they make me feel like a giant is squeezing my head in his fist.

The other kids ran up and asked Minnie questions, like had someone been using a jackhammer too close to her, or had she eaten ice cream too fast? But I wasn't listening, because that's when I noticed Maya.

Chapter 2

Maya was sitting on her lunch box, next to Minnie. Here's what she looked like:

1. Very long black straight hair. Super long. Rapunzel long. Her hair was so long, she was *sitting* on it!

2. On top of her head was a pink winter hat with kitty ears and a nose. I wondered why she was wearing a hat when it was only September and still nice and warm out.

3. She was sitting perfectly still and straight, like she was a statue.

Have No Fear!

So, of course, I was just dying with curiosity about what kind of sickness or trouble she had. I couldn't help but ask, "What's wrong with *you*?"

She blinked at me really sloooowly and didn't say anything. Her eyes were open wide.

"Ummm, can you talk?" I asked her.

She nodded.

"I'm going to guess what's wrong with you, okay?" I asked.

She shrugged.

"You threw up?"

She shook her head no.

"You hit your head?"

More shaking.

So then I tried a whole bunch of guesses in a row.

"You cut your finger or you sprained your ankle or you have a strep throat or an ear infection or you got your appendix removed or you're under the curse of a goblin queen who is forcing you to sit on your lunch box or else she'll eat you for dinner?"

No dice, as my dad says.

I looked closely at Maya then. Her eyes were opened so wide, and they were all wet, too, like she was about to cry.

Have No Fear!

"Are you scared?" I asked.

That's when she nodded really big and fast.

Bingo!

Well, this made me even more curious, of course.

"What are you scared of?"

She just blinked.

"Tornadoes?"

"Vacuum cleaners?"

"Men with beards?"

"Ladies with beards?"

"Bloodsucking vampires?"

"Snakes?"

"Spiders?"

She suddenly started nodding like crazy again.

"You're scared of spiders!" I shouted.

I was so happy to have guessed it. But then I

saw a big, juicy tear slide down her cheek, and I wasn't happy anymore.

"Is that why you're wearing your winter hat? To protect yourself from the spiders?" I asked.

She nodded and pulled her hat down lower on her head.

"But there aren't any spiders here," I said.

Then she whispered something, except it was in such a tiny little voice, I couldn't hear it. So I leaned in reeeeeally close and put my ear right next to her face, and she said it again.

"Not just spiders. All bugs," she whispered.

"Oooooh," I said. She pointed to the garbage can by the fence, and sure enough, there was a big fat bumblebee buzzing around.

"But that bee is so far away!" I said. "He's, like, a hundred miles away from you!"

Have No Fear!

"What if he flies over here?" she whispered.

"Then we'll run away!"

"What if he chases us?"

"We'll run faster!"

"What if he catches up? What if he stings us? What if his stinger falls off and gets stuck in my skin? What if I'm allergic to bumblebees?"

I could tell that she would keep asking what-if questions no matter what. She was that worried.

"Hey, I know!" I said happily. "I'll squash him for you!"

Squashing bugs is one of my talents. I have squashed spiders, mosquitoes, flies, and ants, and once I even squashed an enormous cockroach.

Maya whispered, "But what if another one comes?"

Holy cannoli, was she scared bad. This wasn't

just your usual heebie-jeebies. This was serious. And seeing that tear on her face made me so gloomy, I decided I'd skip tag just this once and cheer her up instead.

I told her all my best jokes. I told her *Why is six scared of seven?* (*Because seven ate nine!*) and *How do you make a tissue dance?* (*Put a little boogey in it!*). Pretty soon she smiled, and then she even laughed a little.

I told her I liked her kitty hat, and she said it

was from Tokyo, which is in Japan. She was born there, and she goes back every summer to see her grandparents. She said she has to ride on a plane for fourteen hours to get there. I couldn't believe it!

Then the whistle blew, which meant recess was over and it was time for lunch. I told her my name super fast and asked what hers was.

"Maya," she whispered.

"Okay, Maya, see you tomorrow! Same time, same place!" Then I grabbed my lunch box and raced over to the red doors, to go in for lunch.

Chapter 3

The next morning, while I was getting ready for school, I had a great idea about how to make Maya feel better. I was going to bring my funny eyeglasses with the big fat nose and furry mustache attached!

I took absolutely everything out of my costume box, but I couldn't find them. So I ran into the kitchen yelling "DA-AD! DA-AD!" and there he was, dressed for success, wearing his tool belt.

My dad is a super. I used to think that was short for *superhero*, but his job actually has nothing to do with superpowers at all, which is really too bad. I would *love* it if my dad could fly or shoot laser beams out of his eyes.

His job is a lot more boring than it sounds. He works at this big apartment building called the Monroe, which is near our school, and he has to fix all the things that break in people's apartments. The coolest part about his job is that he has a lot of tools, like saws and screw guns and drills—but it's not that cool, because he won't let me touch them.

So Dad was wearing his tool belt that I'm not allowed to touch and pouring himself a cup of coffee. I have learned that it is a good idea to let grown-ups drink coffee before you try to talk to them in the morning.

I said, "Have some coffee, Dad."

He took a sip, and I waited for the magic ingredient they put in coffee to work.

Then I asked, "Where are my funny glasses with the big fat nose and furry mustache?"

"Those are mine," Jude said. He was sitting at the table reading *Manga Mania* and eating his yogurt.

Jude is always reading. Or drawing comic books. Or doing crossword puzzles or playing chess or video games. Everything he likes to do is stuff you do sitting down and being quiet. How boring can you get?

Everything I like to do is stuff you do loud and fast, like singing at the top of my lungs or turning three cartwheels in a row or playing with dogs. Jude hates dogs. He thinks they are smelly and gross. Which is exactly what I think about him.

"Those glasses are mine!" I said. "Nana gave them to me for Christmas!"

"Nana gave us *both* a pair," he said, looking very satisfied. "But you wore yours when you were doing handstands, so they broke. The ones that are left are mine. And you can't use them, because you're totally irresponsible."

He thinks he's so great. It makes me furious. It's no wonder I made a poster of him that says:

He made me promise never to reveal what his middle name is, and I keep my promises, even though it would serve him right if I told everyone his middle name was Ba— See? I stopped myself.

"But you can't even wear those funny glasses, because you already wear glasses!" I shouted.

It's true! Jude has worn glasses ever since I can remember. He's nearsighted. That means he can see things that are near to him, but if he doesn't wear his glasses, things that are far away look fuzzy.

He just ignored me, which is the *most* annoying thing he ever does.

Just when I was about to clobber Jude, I heard a tiny high-pitched voice behind me say, "Wonny! Wonny!" That voice could belong to only one person. My favorite person!

My little sister, Pearl, came running into the kitchen. She's two years old. Here's what she looks like:

1. Short blond hair that always looks messy.

2. Big, round blue eyes.

3. A body that's so skinny, her pants are always falling off her butt.

If she were a dog, she'd be a Chihuahua puppy. Jude and I both have the same straight blond hair and blue eyes as Pearl. All three of us look like one another, so sometimes I like to pretend we're triplets. Jude says that's impossible because we are all different ages and triplets all have to be born on the same day. He is what I call a party pooper.

Pearl was holding her favorite stuffed animal, which she sleeps with every night. It's a big black furry rat named Ricardo, only she says it "Wicawdo." Pearl loves rats. She loves rats so much that Dad says he has to be careful when he takes her on the subway because she always wants to pet the rats she sees on the tracks. So for her second birthday, Mom and Dad gave her Ricardo. My grandmother says Ricardo gives her the creeps.

Pearl calls me Wonny, which is her way of saying Ronny, which is a dumb nickname Jude gave to me when I was a poor, defenseless baby. My

Have No Fear!

whole family calls me Ronny, and I just can't stand it. So I told them no one can call me that anymore, except for Pearl because, well, she's so cute and a baby and all.

So Pearl came running into the kitchen calling my name, and what was she holding in her little fist but the funny glasses with the big fat nose and furry mustache!

"My gwasses!" she said, handing them to me.

I had totally forgotten that Nana gave Pearl a pair of glasses for Christmas, too, and that smart little baby knew exactly where they were. You know where she gets her brains from, don't you? Me, of course.

By that time, my dad had drunk enough coffee to be able to talk, so he said, "Okay, so I gotta ask, Ronny Bear—"

But before he could go on, I raised my eyebrows and gave him a look that said, *Dad, we've talked about this about a million times!*

And he said, "Sorry, I meant Veronica. Why do you need your funny glasses for school today?"

"Just helping out a friend in need," I said. "All in a day's work."

"That's what I like to hear," said my mom as she walked into the kitchen. Mom was dressed for success in a flowery skirt and dangly earrings.

Have No Fear!

She's a therapist. I didn't used to know what that meant, but then she explained it to me:

"People come to my office, and they talk to me about their problems and feelings. I help them think of ways to handle their problems or just feel better about them."

"Are you kidding?" I laughed. "Your whole job is to listen to people's problems? That's *so* easy. A kid could do that!"

She laughed at me, but I wasn't even joking.

I'm also kind of an expert on problems from watching TV at Nana and Nonno's apartment. They're my dad's parents, and they live on the top floor of our building.

There are four floors in our building, which is the same building my dad lived in when he was a little boy. The bottom floor is where my mom has her office and sees clients. The second and third floors are where we live. The fourth floor is where Nana and Nonno live.

They are retired. At first I thought the word was *tired*, and I thought it was weird to have a party for someone who's tired. But then my dad explained that being *re*-tired is when you don't have a job anymore because you're old.

When I am sick and stay home from school, I go to Nana and Nonno's apartment, and it is so much fun. I lie on the couch, and Nana treats me like a queen. She brings me soup and tea and juice and Popsicles. And she lets me watch her shows with her.

She loves all kinds of TV shows, but her favorites are what she calls "talk shows," which is weird because every show on TV has talking in it. They should be called "yell shows" or "cry shows" because that's what people do on them. Real people who

have awful problems go on these shows, and the host talks to them about their problems and then gives them advice or sometimes yells stuff at them, like "Get your life together!"

Nana gets all excited, and sometimes she yells at the TV, which I think is just so hilarious.

"Look-a dis guy! What a dummy-a!" she shouts.

Nana comes from Italy, and she has an accent, which I can imitate by just adding *a* to the end of every word, like "My-a name-a is-a Veronica-a!"

So I know a lot about problems because of the talk shows. But when I ask Mom to tell me some of the problems people talk to her about, she absolutely refuses. She says they're private.

"I won't tell anyone," I promise.

She just laughs. She can be really stubborn when she wants to be.

It's her job to help people, and she really likes it when I do that, too. So when she heard I was using the funny glasses to come to the rescue, she seemed really proud, which made me feel great.

Then I stuck the glasses on my face and felt even better because Pearl laughed so hard that milk came out of her nose. I just knew they would work with Maya.

Chapter 4

When recess started, Noah ran up to me and asked if I wanted to play Air Tag. That *is* one of my favorite kinds of tag. It is also the only kind of tag where I can beat Noah, because your feet can't touch the ground. But I really wanted to see if my funny glasses would do the trick to help Maya out. So I said, "Not today, Noah. Have fun without me. But not too much fun, okay?"

Then I raced over lickety-split to the fence, but Maya wasn't there. Know who *was* there? Matthew Sawyer, pressing a paper towel on his knee.

Matthew Sawyer is my sworn enemy. If you see

him, watch out! He looks like a perfectly innocent person, but as my mom says, looks can be deceiving. Here's how you will know it's him:

1. Always wearing striped shirts. Never up-and-down stripes. Always sideways.

2. Shoelaces that are always untied.

3. No front teeth. Well, hardly any. His top two front teeth fell out, and then a few days later, so did two of his bottom teeth. He is so proud of his jack-o'-lantern smile. He is always sticking his tongue in his tooth hole just because I don't like it.

4. Brown hair that is so super short that it looks like a fuzzy, comfy carpet on his head. This hairstyle is called a buzz cut. I know that because last year, Jude had lice three times in a row, and Dad

finally just shaved his hair into a buzz cut. I asked Matthew Sawyer if he'd also had lice, and he said, "No, but that would be so cool! Can you bring me a louse?" Can you *believe* that?

I have been in Matthew Sawyer's class for three years in a row, and every year, he drives me nuts. If Matthew Sawyer were a dog, he would be a basset hound. They never stop barking.

So there was Matthew Sawyer, sitting by the fence with a hurt knee. Even though I should have known better, I asked him, "What happened to you?"

"Oh, this?" he asked, looking down at his knee. "Just my flesh-eating bacteria acting up again."

Matthew Sawyer's mom is a doctor, and she tells him all about weird germs, so he is an expert on gross medical problems.

"I am not falling for that again," I told him.
"What is it really?"

"Bloodsucking hookworms."

I rolled my eyes.

"Rabies."

"Oh, for crying out loud!" I exclaimed. "I know
you just scraped your knee!"

"I did," he admitted. "On a rhinoceros toenail.
With fungus on it."

I sighed really loudly, and then I asked, "Do
you know where Maya is?"

Have No Fear!

"Why?" he asked.

He smiled, but it wasn't a friendly smile that said, *How can I help you?* It was a devilish smile that said, *How can I make lots of trouble for you?*

"None of your beeswax," I said.

"If you don't tell me why, then I won't tell you where she is."

I growled a little, and then I sighed, and then I said, "Because she's scared, and I have something that can help!"

"Oh," he said. "Sounds boring."

"Well, where is she?"

"How should I know?" he said. "I don't even know who Maya is."

Oooooh, that Matthew Sawyer is the worst thing since the invention of homework! I really wanted to give him a shove, but I knew he'd tattle on me. So I just took a deep breath and kept looking for Maya.

The Fix-It Friends

I ran through the soccer games and the basketball games and the monkey bars, but she wasn't anywhere.

So finally I did something I *really* don't like to do. I went over to Miss Tibbs, who is the recess teacher. The reason I don't like to do that is because Miss

Tibbs is super strict. If you go near her, you'll end up in trouble for doing nothing at all! Here are all the things Miss Tibbs has scolded me for:

1. Not tying my shoelaces.
2. Wiping my nose on my sleeve because I didn't have a tissue.
3. Eating the cookies in Minnie's lunch (even though she didn't want them!).

4. Throwing balls at Matthew Sawyer's back (even though he was throwing the balls at me first).

5. Running too fast.

6. Walking too slow.

7. Yelling too loud. ("Are you trying to wake the dead?" she said.)

8. Laughing too loud. ("Are you trying to give me a migraine?" she said.)

9. Whispering too loud. ("I can hear everything you're saying about me, Miss Conti. If you're going to whisper, you'd better learn how to do it correctly.")

I don't mean to be mean, but she looks like a witch from a fairy tale. She has thick gray hair that is as long as her ears. She wears big black glasses, and her face is always in a scowl.

And she always wears black! I'm not kidding. Even on Valentine's Day and Saint Patrick's Day and stuff. It's spooky.

So I reeeeeeally do not like to talk to Miss Tibbs. But I just couldn't find Maya anywhere, so I had no choice.

I said, "Hey, Miss Tibbs, do you know where Maya is?"

"Hay is for horses," she said. It's what she always says. Usually, I try to explain to her that it's a different kind of hay, but on this day I didn't have the time.

"Okay," I said. "But do you know where she is?"

"Do you mean the Maya you were talking to yesterday? Miss Tanaka?"

I nodded.

Have No Fear!

Miss Tibbs knows *everything* that happens at recess. Absolutely everything. If a kid drops a candy wrapper in the most faraway corner of the playground, she knows it, and she marches right over to make him pick it up. If a kid is saying something mean, even in a whisper, she hears it, and she gives that kid a piece of her mind.

"Miss Tanaka is quite upset today. She was so upset that she decided to stay inside at recess. She's in the office."

"No!" I gasped.

"Yes," Miss Tibbs said.

"NO!!" I gasped again.

Then Miss Tibbs tipped her chin down and gave me a look that said, *Come on, now, you're overdoing it.*

So I said, "Can I go see her? Please? PLEASE!"

Miss Tibbs thought about it for a second. She

made her eyes really narrow while she was thinking, so she looked even scarier than usual.

Then she said, "You know, I think a dose of Veronica Laverne Conti might be just what Miss Tanaka needs. Go ahead."

I grabbed my lunch box and raced through the red double doors of my school. I was in total disbelief.

Miss Tibbs knew my middle name? How on earth did she find that out? She really did have magic powers.

Chapter 5

The school office is a huge room with a lot of ladies in it talking on phones and typing on computers and looking pretty grumpy. There are some chairs in the office for if you are late or if you are early or if you are in big trouble and have to go see the principal. Principal Powell has a little office inside the big office, with a door that closes. There are no windows in that door, so you have no idea what is going on in there.

Sitting at a desk in front of Principal Powell's office is Mrs. Rose Mackenzie ... or is it Mrs. Mackenzie Rose? Both her names sound like first names so I can't remember which comes first. She is the grumpiest one of all the office ladies. She is almost 100 years old, and her hair is completely white. I think she used to be a librarian because she is always *shh*ing everyone.

The office is a very boring place. There are no kids' books or magazines and no pads of paper and crayons. There is no TV with cartoons playing. There is absolutely nothing fun or interesting about it.

I really could not believe that Maya chose to spend her whole recess there. First she was sitting by the fence and now this? I just had to help her.

When I got there, I saw Maya sitting on her princess hair, right there in front of Principal Powell's office. That part didn't surprise me.

What surprised me was that Jude was sitting next to her. They looked very chummy. He had his

head bent down to talk to her because she was so tiny and he was so tall.

"Jude!" I screeched. "What on earth did you do? Why'd you get sent to the principal's office?"

Jude looked up and glowered at me. I love that word because it sounds like exactly what it is. His blue eyes got all glimmery because he was so mad.

"I wasn't sent to the principal's office," he said. "I'm helping Maya out."

I was in total disbelief again.

"But I'm helping her out!" I shouted.

"Can I talk to you privately?" Jude said in a low voice. There he went again, acting like a grown-up. He grabbed my hand and pulled me into the hallway.

"What are you doing here?" I asked.

"I'm a recess mediator, remember? I'm on mediator duty today."

"Yeah, but that just means you are supposed to stop kids from clobbering each other."

"Actually, it means I'm supposed to help kids at recess with any of their problems," he said, pushing up his glasses. They are always sliding down his nose. "Maya needs help, big-time. She's so terrified of bugs, she won't even go outside."

"I already know *all* about this," I said, very impatiently. "But she was outside yesterday! So what happened?"

Have No Fear!

"This morning, she saw a spider on her walk to school, and she totally freaked out."

"But Jude—" I hollered.

"*Shhhh!*" He glowered again. "You're going to get us sent to the principal's office for real!"

"But Jude!" I whispered. "This is a disaster. Recess is the best part of the day! She can't miss it!"

He nodded. "That's why I'm helping her."

I had to laugh. I couldn't help it. How ridiculous!

"I'm the people person around here. Let me handle this," I said. He didn't look convinced, so I said, "Miss Tibbs told me to!"

Jude groaned. "Fine. We'll do it together," he said, walking back into the office. "Just try not to make things worse."

Chapter 6

Jude and I tried everything to cheer Maya up.

First, I put on my funny glasses with the big nose and furry mustache.

"TA-DA!" I shouted.

Mrs. Rose/Mackenzie and the other office ladies said "*Shhh!!*" at the same exact time.

But Maya didn't laugh. She didn't even crack a tiny smile.

Jude tried talking to Maya in his I'm-a-big-stinky-grown-up way.

"Bugs are more scared of you than you are of them," he said.

Have No Fear!

Then I told her about when I got a spider bite last summer in Texas when we went to visit Mom's parents, Granny and Gramps: "It only itched for a day, and then it went away, and it was no big deal."

Then Jude said we should try to take her mind off bugs and talk about other stuff instead. So he drew a comic strip about a superhero named Super Maya.

I would never tell this to Jude, but he draws the best comics. They look really professional. He

makes up the funniest characters. Usually they are animals that act like humans. Like a detective pig or a raccoon that does karate.

I don't know how he can draw such good expressions on their faces, but he can really make them look scared or excited or confused or whatever he wants. He even made Super Maya's long black hair flow in the air as she flew.

"Look," I laughed. "Maya can fly-a!"

But Maya just gave us a tiny little smile like she was being polite. She really couldn't get her mind off her troubles.

I got so desperate to make her laugh that I stood on my head, which turned out to be a big mistake. I lost my balance and I accidentally knocked over the humongous tin can that says PENNIES FOR THE RAIN FOREST on it.

Every year, all the kids in the whole school

bring in all the pennies they can find and drop them in the can. Then Principal Powell gives the money to save the Amazon rain forest. She usually empties out the can before summer break, but I guess she forgot or didn't have time, because it was still full on the second day of school. Not just full. Overflowing!

When I kicked the penny can, four billion pennies spilled all over the office floor. It made the most enormous racket you have ever heard. I'm not even kidding. Principal Powell came running out of her office with this scared expression on her face and a half-eaten sandwich in her hand.

But before she could say a word, I heard Miss Tibbs's voice from the doorway behind me.

"I'll take care of it."

Then Principal Powell walked back into her office and Miss Tibbs turned to me.

"Miss Conti," she said. "I expect you to pick up every one of those pennies."

"But it—" I started to say.

"No buts," said Miss Tibbs. She was holding her finger up close to my face like she meant business. "You have exactly three minutes before you need to be in the lunchroom. Recess is over."

I gave Jude my best puppy dog look, which said,

Have No Fear!

Please help me! I'm just a poor defenseless little sister after all!

So he did, and Maya helped, too, and I got to lunch on time.

One thing was for sure. Well, two things.

1. A person shouldn't do headstands outside the principal's office.

2. If Jude and I were going to help Maya, we needed some help ourselves.

Chapter 7

That night, Dad made spaghetti and meatballs. Dad is a terrific cook. He cooks Italian food mostly because that's what Nana always made when he was a kid.

That's fine by me because I love macaroni. You can put anything on macaroni, and it will taste delicious. Sometimes he puts eggs and bacon on it. He calls it breakfast macaroni even though we eat it for dinner. But spaghetti and meatballs is my all-time favorite meal. Especially with extra Parmesan cheese.

Pearl hardly eats anything at dinnertime, but

even she likes it when we have spaghetti. She doesn't eat much of the noodles, but she sure loves the sauce. She sucks all the sauce off her spaghetti until her face is all dirty and the spaghetti is all clean.

Jude and I were telling Mom and Dad about Maya's problem. But I had a problem of my own. Which was that Jude wouldn't even let me tell my own story!

Jude told Mom and Dad, "It was my job to help Maya, but then Ronny just barged in and knocked over about a million pennies and got us all in trouble."

I gasped. "Outrageous!"

Jude kept going. "If I wasn't there to help her clean it up, who knows what Miss Tibbs would have done to her."

Besides hogging my story, Jude was hogging

the cheese. How could I eat my spaghetti and meatballs without a whole pile of Parmesan cheese on top? So I grabbed the cheese out of his hands, but I grabbed it a little too hard, and the cheese went flying over my shoulder all over the rug. Not only that, but when I grabbed it, I accidentally knocked over Jude's glass of water so that it spilled right onto the table—and onto the floor, too.

Have No Fear!

He howled like he was a bear and I had stepped on his big bear paw.

I opened my eyes wide and blinked slowly, which is my *I'm so sweet and innocent* face. I learned it from Cora. It's what her face always looks like.

"Oopsy daisy," I said.

"Oopsy daisy!" repeated Pearl from her high chair. She repeats absolutely everything, which is so funny, except when she repeats bad words. To be honest, I think that's the funniest of all, but my parents don't. They raise their eyebrows and say, "Oh no, no, Pearl! That's not a nice word at all!"

She must've really liked the way *oopsy daisy* sounded, because she started saying it over and over again: "Oopsy daisy, oopsy daisy, oopsy oopsy oopsy daisy!" She had spaghetti sauce all over her face, which made it even funnier.

I couldn't help but giggle, and my giggling just made her do it more.

"Don't encourage her," my mom scolded. But it was too late.

"OOPSY DAISY! OOPSY DAISY!! OOOO-OOO—" Pearl shouted at the top of her lungs.

I was laughing so loud, I snorted. That made Pearl laugh, too.

"It's not funny!" Jude yelled.

"NOT FUNNY!" Pearl screamed. She scrunched up her little face to imitate his mad face.

My dad blew on his fingers to make a whistle sound. I don't know how he does that, but it's really cool. Kind of almost like a superpower.

Then Jude and I wiped up the water, and after we'd finished eating, Dad got out the vacuum cleaner to suck up the cheese from the rug.

Have No Fear!

"But Dad!" I said. "You-know-who doesn't like you-know-what!"

Pearl is absolutely terrified of the vacuum cleaner. Imagine if the bogeyman and a werewolf and a brain-gobbling zombie were all rolled into one. Now imagine how terrified you'd be if you saw that creature in your living room. That is how Pearl looks every time Mom or Dad takes out the vacuum cleaner.

I thought maybe Dad forgot about this. But he said, "Yep, I know she's scared of the vacuum, kiddo. But if we keep her away from it, she'll never stop being scared. She has to face her fear."

"Sounds like you're trying to torture a poor little baby to me," I said.

My mom piped up. "I think it was Eleanor Roosevelt who said, 'Do one thing that scares you every day.'"

My mom loves quoting famous people. It's her favorite hobby.

"You mean, Eleanor Roosevelt wants me to hug a shark today? And climb in a volcano tomorrow?" I joked.

"She didn't say, 'Do something really dumb every day,'" said Jude.

At just that moment, Pearl saw the vacuum and her eyes got enormously big. Her lower lip started to tremble.

"No vakzoom, Daddy! I NO LIKE DAT VAKZOOM!"

Dad told her we had to use the vacuum but she could go into the other room if it was too loud. So she ran into her bedroom as fast as her little legs could carry her. She gets to have her own bedroom, and I have to share one with Jude, which kind of

Have No Fear!

isn't fair. But her room is so teeny tiny, it is more like a closet than a room, and I don't think all my stuffed animals would fit in there. Plus, our room is upstairs next to my parents' bedroom, which makes me feel safer when I go to bed. So I'm really not that jealous.

Pearl stayed in her room for a minute, but then she walked into the hall and peeked out around the corner.

"Vakzoom too WOUD!"

"Yep. It is loud," said my dad as he sucked up all the cheese. "You can say, 'Quiet down, vacuum!'"

"BE QUIET, YOU NAUGHTY VAKZOOM!" she shouted.

Then we all laughed and she laughed, too. So she said it again and again, and she even came out into the living room and shouted it right at the vacuum.

"Pearl!" I shrieked as I gave her a giant hug. "You did it! You're not afraid of the vacuum anymore!"

"Well, it's probably not as simple as that," said my mom, "but it's definitely a step in the right direction." She was putting strawberries and whipped cream into bowls for dessert.

"It's just like when you were Pearl's age, and you were scared of going down the drain in the bathtub," Dad said to me.

Have No Fear!

"Me? Scared of the bath?" I snorted. "I love baths! I'm practically a mermaid."

"No, Dad's right! I remember that!" Jude said. He was cutting his berries in half with a knife and fork instead of just popping them into his mouth like a normal person. "You were so scared. Mom bought you every kind of bubble bath and rubber ducky and stuff, but you refused to get in the bath for weeks!"

He laughed so hard, he doubled over.

I really, really wanted to grab the whipped cream and spray it in Jude's big laughing face.

But that seemed like a waste of good whipped cream. So I squirted that cream into my bowl instead. The only thing I love more than extra cheese is extra whipped cream.

"Then, one day, I just tossed you in the tub," Dad said. "You cried for a minute, but then I made your windup scuba diver swim, and you calmed down. After a few days like that, you were pretty much over your terror of baths."

I stood up really fast then and shouted, "BINGO!"

"BINGO!" shouted Pearl.

"What is it?" Mom asked.

"I think I know just how to solve Maya's problem!"

I shoved the rest of the berries and cream in my mouth real fast so I could get to work in my bedroom.

"Uh-oh," Jude groaned. "I don't think I like the sound of this."

Chapter 8

The next day, at the beginning of recess, Minnie told me she had seen Maya walking into the office with her lunch box. So I ran right up to Miss Tibbs and asked if I could go see Maya in the office. Cora came with me.

"Do you plan on knocking over an entire can of pennies?" Miss Tibbs asked me.

"Nope," I said. Of course, I didn't plan on it last time. It just happened. Things like that just happen to me sometimes.

Miss Tibbs looked at me for a second and frowned. Then Cora piped up.

"I'd be happy to go with her, Miss Tibbs!" squeaked Cora. "I went to preschool with Maya, and I think I can help. With your permission, of course."

Grown-ups love Cora. It's like she puts an enchanted spell on them with her cuteness. Here are the ingredients of the spell:

1. Squeaky voice.

2. Bouncy red curls.

3. Polka-dot dresses that are always very tidy and never have any rips or chocolate stains on them.

All these things make her seem sweeter than a double-fudge brownie with whipped cream on top. But the secret ingredient is:

4. Perfect manners.

Not just "please" and "thank you" but "if you insist" and "pardon me." Her twin sister, Camille,

doesn't have these manners, so I don't know where Cora got them from. But what I do know is they work like magic to get grown-ups to do what she wants. Including Miss Tibbs.

When Cora started talking, Miss Tibbs's grumpy expression melted into a peaceful one. Her eyebrows un-scrunched. Her frown really and truly turned upside down! It wasn't quite a smile, but it was as close as Miss Tibbs gets. I have never seen Miss Tibbs really smile. I don't think it is actually possible.

"Thank you, Miss Klein, for the kind offer," Miss Tibbs said. "You may both go. Just be sure there are no disasters this time."

"Absolutely, Miss Tibbs," Cora squeaked. "Thank you very much!"

We grabbed our lunch boxes. I peeked inside mine to make sure the special surprise was still in there. Then we zoomed over to the office.

Jude wasn't there, because it wasn't one of his recess mediator days. What a relief.

Jude's best friend, Ezra, was there, though. Ezra is so nice. If he were my brother, instead of Jude, I bet we would never fight. We'd just hold hands and skip around happily like elves. Here's what Ezra looks like:

1. Braces! He was the first person I know to get braces, and they are so fascinating. He can't eat corn on the

cob or taffy anymore, and he can't ride bumper cars! Plus he has rubber bands in his mouth. Real, true rubber bands! And he says he got to pick the colors.

2. Huge brown eyes with very long eyelashes.

3. Brown hair that is super curly and fluffy. Cora has big curls, but Ezra has little ones. For my birthday last year, I asked Mom and Dad to buy me a set of little pink foam hair curlers. I really thought they'd make my hair as curly as Ezra's. But Mom said I had to sleep with them on my head, and how can a person sleep with a whole bunch of rollers itching her like crazy all night? So they didn't work.

The Fix-It Friends

Ezra was walking into the principal's office, but it wasn't because he was in trouble. It was because the principal is his mom! I wish my mom were the principal. Then I could rule the school. I'd go on the loudspeaker all the time and make announcements like "Matthew Sawyer, you are in big trouble for being a rotten old stink-bag. Report to my mom's office IMMEDIATELY!"

Ezra never does stuff like that, which I think is a waste of his good fortune.

"Hi, Ezra!" I said.

"Hi, Ronny," he said back. Even though I don't like that nickname, I don't mind so much when Ezra says it, because Ezra is very kind to me. He always lets me play with Jude and him, even when Jude yells, "Get outta here, you pest!" I think he appreciates little sisters because he is an only child and doesn't have any of his own. He has a guinea pig named Ziggy, but it's not the same thing.

Ezra's mom is super nice, too. She is from Jamaica, so she has a way of talking that makes everything seem like a song. Ezra does not talk like that. He has a way of talking that makes everything he says seem like a hurricane. He talks super, super fast.

"Oh hey, listen," he said. I did get ready to listen because when Ezra talks, you have to pay close attention. "I'm probably coming to your house after school today with Jude because I thought I had computer class but it doesn't start for a few weeks so I'm about to ask my mom if I can go home with Jude because we're making a new movie and we're kind of at the most crucial scene."

He can say a whole bunch of sentences in the same time it takes regular people to say just a few words. Sometimes all his words blur together and

The Fix-It Friends

I don't know what on earth he's talking about. But since he has been Jude's best friend for so long, I've gotten good at understanding him.

Ezra talks fast but he types faster. He is a computer whiz. He can make up his own video games and movies and music. Ezra loves music, just like me. The only difference is, I like popular songs that play on the radio, and Ezra likes music from the olden days before we were born. He and his mom even have an old-fashioned record player that works and everything.

When he comes over, here's what Ezra and Jude do:

1. Make scary movies about funny things like evil parakeets.
2. Play video games.
3. Read comic books.

Have No Fear!

4. Eat nachos they make in the micro-
wave.

I think video games and comic books are really
boring, but I do like nachos. I also like being in
their movies because I always get to be the Scream
Queen. This is the girl who screams bloodcurdling
screams of terror. Ezra says there is always one in
every scary movie.

"Okay, see you later!" I told Ezra as he went into his mom's office. Then Cora and I turned to Maya.

Cora gave Maya a little wave. Maya gave a little wave back.

"Mind if we sit down?" I asked oh-so-innocently.

"Okay," Maya whispered. She had her hair in a long black braid down her back. I thought of how fun it would be to snip the braid off and wear it on my head. No matter how much I try, I can never grow my hair long like that. I wondered if Maya's mom gave her special vitamins to make her hair grow long. I wanted to ask right then, but I figured first we should take care of business.

So I sat down in the empty chair next to her, and Cora sat down next to me. I hummed a little song, just to show how everything was hunky-dory. I put my lunch box on my lap. It is a super-cool lunch box. The front is all blue with a poodle wearing earmuffs and ice-skating.

I slowly unzipped my lunch box . . . and then I shrieked.

Right there was the world's most enormous spider. It was as big as my hand and very black with furry legs. It was sitting right on top of my cream-cheese-and-jelly sandwich.

"A spider!" I shrieked. Well, I pretended to shriek. Of course, I had known the spider was in there the whole time. I put it there myself. And it wasn't a real spider, just a fake one from last Halloween. But it doesn't look fake at all.

I looked over at Maya really fast to see what she would do.

She didn't jump up. In fact, she didn't even move a muscle. She just opened her eyes really, really, really big. And she screamed.

The Fix-It Friends

You know how in the cartoons when someone screams super loud, all the glass in the windows break?

That is how loud she screamed. Maybe even louder.

I think I'm a great Scream Queen, but the sound that came out of Maya's mouth was a hundred times louder than even my best scream.

Principal Powell and Ezra came running into the room. She must have been in the middle of eating lunch because she was holding a thermos of soup in one hand and a spoon in the other. Well, she ran so fast, the thermos of soup splashed all over her clothes and onto the floor. And I guess that made the floor really slippery, because before I knew it, she was yelling, "Ahhhh!" and Ezra was saying, "Mom! Watch out!" while she fell backward onto her butt. Which made the soup splash everywhere.

Meanwhile, Maya just kept right on screaming. I didn't even know how she could breathe, because her scream lasted so long. She was like an opera singer!

Cora is a fast thinker. She snatched the spider out of my lunch box and yelled, "It's fake! It's

fake!" but Maya probably couldn't even hear her, because she was yelling so loud.

All sorts of people came running into the office. The school nurse came and the custodian and even my own teacher, Miss Mabel. And, of course, Miss Tibbs, too.

Mrs. Rose/Mackenzie helped Principal Powell up. The other grown-ups crowded around Maya. I was absolutely frozen in place. How can a person think with all that noise?

Finally, Cora said, "Look! I'm taking the fake spider out of here!" and she walked out of the office with it. Then Maya stopped screaming and started crying instead.

I felt awful. I felt worse than awful. I felt even worse than the time I'd accidentally whacked Pearl in the leg with the mini golf club when I was trying to get a hole in one.

Have No Fear!

I was only trying to help Maya, the same way my dad had helped Pearl and me by making us face our fears. I thought if she just saw a bug, right up close, she wouldn't be scared anymore.

The nurse took Maya into her office, and everybody else went back to work, except for Miss Tibbs, who marched me right into the principal's office.

Principal Powell was really nice about the whole thing. It helped that Ezra defended me.

"Mom, she didn't mean to scare her. Well, she *did* mean to, but only because she really wants to help," Ezra said super fast. "Her heart was in the right place."

Principal Powell sighed.

"Your heart is always in the right place, Veronica," she said. "It's your big ideas that get you in trouble sometimes."

I felt so bad about how I'd made Maya cry that I started crying a little bit, too.

"It's all right," Principal Powell said. "But how about you give Maya some space for a few days, okay?"

I nodded.

Then Principal Powell handed me a tissue and sent me to lunch. Cora was waiting for me in the hallway, and she squeezed my hand all the way to the cafeteria.

Chapter 9

That night, Dad made sloppy Joes, only he calls them sloppy Giovannis because he's Italian and he's funny.

Sloppy Giovannis are the super-supreme best. I mean, you're *allowed* to be messy when you eat them because, well, look what they're named! And if you think regular people are sloppy when they eat sloppy Joes, just imagine what Pearl looks like! She gets the sauce all over her face and hands and even her *hair*.

"Oh, you're my cute little Pearly Pig!" I usually say to her.

But I was feeling so lousy about Maya that I didn't smile when I saw Pearl rub her sloppy Giovanni on her belly. I didn't even touch my juicy sandwich.

"What's up, Ronny?" Mom said. "You look blue."

"Nothing," I mumbled. I was so down in the dumps, I didn't even tell her not to call me Ronny.

"Awww, don't worry about what happened with Maya today," Ezra said. He always stays for dinner when we have sloppy Giovannis.

Have No Fear!

"What happened with Maya today?" Mom asked.

"Didn't Ronny tell you she got sent to the principal's office?" Jude asked.

"Would you put a lid on it!" I growled.

I was so furious, I stormed into my room and slammed the door. Then a few seconds later, I opened the door again but just to tape up my sign that said:

I made the sign a long time ago. It was Mom's

idea. She said I should use it when I was blazing mad and needed some time to myself.

I practiced handstands against the wall for a while. Then I put on my pajamas and took out all my stuffed dogs to line them up on my bed, which is the bottom bunk. I have seventeen of them. Most are bulldogs because they're my favorite breed, but I have other kinds, too, like a cute white poodle and a gigantic golden retriever.

Then Mom knocked on the door.

"Permission to enter?" she said, like we were in a spaceship.

"Permission granted," I said back.

She sat next to me on my bed and gave me a big hug, and I told her the whole story. Mom is great at listening to my problems. That's because listening is pretty much all she does all day long, so she gets lots of practice.

I tried not to cry, but I did when I got to the
part about how Maya had to go to the nurse's
office. Going to the nurse's office is even worse
than sitting by the fence at recess. It is even worse
than going to the principal's office. I don't know
for sure, but I think the place is full of shots. At
least when you go to the doctor's office, they give
you stickers. The nurse doesn't even have stickers
or lollipops or anything good!

When I thought about Maya sitting in those little blue chairs in there, all because of me, I felt so awful that I had to cry.

Mom twirled my hair around her finger. I love when she does that. I find it oh-so-relaxing. Mom says I used to do it to myself when I was a baby sucking on my pacifier.

"When Pearl faced her fear of the vacuum cleaner, she stopped being scared," I sniffed. "So how come it didn't work with Maya?"

"So that's what you were up to with the spider, huh?" Mom asked.

I gulped and nodded.

"Well, here's the thing, honey. You're right that Maya probably needs to face her fear," said Mom. "But she needs to do it one teeny-tiny baby step at a time. And she has to decide to do it herself. You can't force her or trick her into it."

Have No Fear!

"But she'll never do it unless I force her!" I groaned.

"Well, she might not be ready to jump into a pit of tarantulas—"

That made me laugh. Where would we even find a tarantula pit?

Mom went on. "But I bet she'd be ready to draw a picture of a spider. Or read a book about a friendly spider, like *Charlotte's Web*."

This didn't sound half bad.

"Go on," I said.

"Then, once Maya does something easy like that, she could try something a little harder. She could look at a photograph of a spider and then maybe watch a video of one. Then, later, she could try to hold a fake spider, but just a stuffed one that didn't look real. Baby steps. You get it?"

I did! I *totally* did.

I threw my arms around good old Mom.

"Mom, you're a genius!" I yelled. "I'm going to write Maya a letter right now and say I'm sorry and tell her my plan!"

Mom laughed and said, "I like the enthusiasm, but you need to give Maya some space right now so she can calm down. So it's okay to write a letter, but don't give it to her for a few days."

"Okay, sure," I said as I jumped up to get my markers and glitter and special stationery with puppies wearing sunglasses on the top.

Here's the first letter I wrote to Maya:

I didn't mean to scare you half to death. Well, I did, but in a good way! Don't worry. I won't make you jump in a pit of tarantulas. Ha! That was a joke.

Have No Fear!

I crumpled up that letter and tried again:

Sorry I scared the living daylights out of you. Hey, you're really good at screaming. Have you ever thought of singing in an opera?

That didn't seem right, either. I decided to keep it short and sweet:

I'm really sorry I scared you. I won't do it ever again. If you want me to help you fight your fear with teeny-tiny baby steps, I will but only if you want to. It's your choice.

Sorry again.

p.s. How do you grow your hair so long? Do you take special vitamins?

Chapter 10

I didn't see Maya the whole rest of the week, because she stayed in the office at recess, and I'm kind of banned from there for . . . well, maybe forever.

Then, on Monday, at recess, I was absolutely dying of thirst because Backwards Tag really gives you a workout. So I ran to the water fountain, and I saw Maya sitting by the fence again.

She was wearing her kitty hat, with her hair hanging down. I wished she had her hair in two ponytails. I bet they would look like the tails on giant black stallions.

When she saw me, her eyes got round, and she

scootched back a little, like she was afraid I would bite her.

I held my hands up in the air, open wide. Just like bad guys do in the movies when the police go near them.

"No fake spiders, see?" I joked. She didn't laugh.

"Oh! I have something for you!" I reached into the pocket of my jeans where I had put the letter, and I handed it to her.

Then I said, "I will now leave you alone while you read it."

So I turned my back to her and waited. I twiddled my thumbs.

"Are you done yet?" I asked, turning around for just a second.

She shook her head.

So I turned back around and hummed a little tune to myself. Matthew Sawyer ran by. When

he saw me, he stopped and asked, "Why are you humming?"

"Why shouldn't I?" I asked back.

"Why shouldn't I?" he copied me.

If I wrote a book of all the annoying things Matthew Sawyer does, it would be about a thousand pages long. But the *most* annoying thing is when he copies me.

"Cut it out!" I shrieked.

"Cut it out!" he shrieked.

"Matthew Sawyer, I am going to clobber you."

"Matthew Sawyer, I am going to clobber you."

Have No Fear!

And I was, too. I didn't even care if Miss Tibbs yelled at me. But thankfully, that's just when Maya said, "I'm done."

I spun around to face her.

"So?" I said. "Do you forgive me?"

"Okay," she said.

"Yippee-ki-yay!" I hollered.

"I liked what you said in your letter about little baby steps. I think I could do that."

"Really?" I was shocked.

She nodded. "Yes. 'Cause I'm getting really sick and tired of sitting on my lunch box. It's so boring."

"Of COURSE it is!" I shouted.

"But it has to be tiny baby steps," Maya said.

"Even smaller than baby steps!" I said. "Tiny mouse steps! Tiny ant steps!"

"Umm, Veronica?" Maya said. "You're kind of talking about bugs again."

"Oopsy daisy!" I giggled.

She giggled, too.

Jude and Ezra saw us laughing. They got nosy and just *had* to see what was happening.

"Veronica's going to help me stop being scared of bugs," Maya said.

"Are you sure that's a good idea?" Jude said, raising his eyebrows way up.

Have No Fear!

I glowered at him.

"Okay, okay. That's awesome, Maya," said Jude. He gave her a pat on the back. "You should make a list of all the little steps you're going to take."

I rolled my eyes. Jude loves making lists. Sometimes he even makes lists of the lists he wants to write. I am not kidding!

"I can help if you want," he said.

"Oh, we don't need any help!" I said really fast.

"I could do it on my computer," said Ezra. Then he cracked his knuckles, and I knew he was getting a great idea. When he gets excited, he always cracks his knuckles. "I could make it like a game, with a girl character that looks like you, and—Oh! I know! Every time she does a step, I can make a little animation, with music and everything!"

I was about to tell them "Thanks but no thanks," except Maya was already nodding and saying, "Oh yeah! That'd be fun!" She had a big smile on her face. And she was in charge, after all.

So I put a fake smile on and forced myself to say, "Sure, you can help. The more, the merrier."

Chapter 11

The next day, Maya came over after school so we could make her special list. Ezra brought his laptop. Jude made snacks—nachos with extra Cheddar cheese and sour cream. He and Ezra call this dish the Sour Power. I made drinks: my world-famous specialty called Rama-Lama-Ding-Dongs! Here's what's in it:

1. A little lemonade.

2. A little orange juice.

3. A little seltzer.

4. A maraschino cherry on top.

You can *absolutely* not make it without the cherry. Don't even try.

Jude, who is Mr. List Guy, said we should make the list in the shape of a staircase.

"It's like what Mom always says: 'The journey of a thousand miles begins with a single step.'"

"No offense, but that doesn't even make any sense," I told him. I poured myself another Rama-Lama-Ding-Dong.

"Sure it does," said Ezra, munching nachos. "It just means that you can do really hard things by taking it one step at a time."

"Ohhhhh, I get it," I said, popping extra cherries in my drink. "Like when we had dinner at Dad's friends' house, and I was starving half to death, and all they had to eat was broccoli and pot roast. And I had no choice but to accept my fate and chew up that awful broccoli, one piece at a time."

"You don't like broccoli?" asked Maya. "I love it. It makes me feel like I'm a giant eating trees."

Have No Fear!

I looked at her like she had three heads. Next she was probably going to tell me she did extra homework, just for fun.

Ezra started making the list on his computer. He made it in the shape of a staircase, and on every step, he typed one thing Maya was going to do to face her fear. This time, we let Maya choose what to do.

At the bottom were easy steps, like "Tell a funny story about a spider." The ones up at the top of the staircase were hard, like "Watch a video of a real spider." The last one, at the very tippity top, was "Go see a spider in real life."

Then Ezra made a cartoon Super Maya wearing a red cape and a black mask. Every time she went up on a new step, she raised her hands in the air like a champion, and her cape fluttered.

"It's so cool!" Maya giggled.

The Fix-It Friends

Then I had a great idea to make the bottom of the staircase look like a dark, miserable swamp with rain clouds and crocodiles. But as Super Maya went up the stairs, it looked more and more pretty.

"And at the very top, she can be on a mountain with rainbows and flowers and lollipops," I said. I was on a roll.

"And kittens and cupcakes!" giggled Maya.

"And zombies and mutant vegetables!" said Jude, but he was just teasing.

Go see a spider in real life.

Watch a video of a real spider.

Look at a toy spider.

Tell a funny story about a spider.

Draw a spider.

Have No Fear!

As we talked, Ezra typed on his computer. He hummed while he worked, which I find oh-so-relaxing. In just a few minutes, the staircase list looked exactly like we'd described.

Maya didn't want to get started doing her steps until the next week. So for the rest of the afternoon, we played. She wanted to be a princess. I wanted to be the princess's pet pit bull. Pearl wanted to be the pit bull's pet flea.

"Me the FWEA! Me the FWEA!" she shouted.

Then she found the funny glasses with the big fat nose and furry mustache and put them on. Maya and I laughed so hard we couldn't even breathe.

"Fwea so funny!" Pearl said. She was terribly proud of herself.

Chapter 12

The next Monday, Maya was so excited to come over again to play and do the first step on her chart. Cora came, too.

First, I made Rama-Lama-Ding-Dongs with extra cherries. Then we got down to work. I had thought it would be easy-peasy for Maya to draw a picture of a spider. But it wasn't at all. Maya was reeeeeally scared.

"When I think about bugs, my stomach starts to hurt and my heart starts to thump and it feels awful," she said.

Have No Fear!

"Aw, come on! You can do it!" I said. "It can't jump off the page and bite you!"

But Cora squeaked, "Let's just take a break and have a powdered doughnut."

My dad says powdered doughnuts are his weakness. He tries to hide them from us, but I know when he gets a box of them because I see white powder, which looks like snow, on the counter. Then I yell, "Aha! Powder alert!" and I hunt around in the kitchen until I find where he has hidden them.

After she ate three mini doughnuts, Maya suddenly blurted out, "Okay. I can do it." And she drew a big, hairy spider in permanent marker. It was as big as my hand. It had googly eyes.

"What should we name it?" asked Cora. "Something funny."

"I don't know," said Maya. She was scrunching up her eyebrows and looking nervous again.

"Let's call her . . . Snookums!" I exclaimed. Then I pretended to shriek. "Ahhhh! Snookums is naked!"

That made Maya and Cora laugh so hard, they fell over. It reminded me of what my dad says: "Laughter is the best medicine." It's true!

"Let's dress Snookums!" said Cora. "We'll give her a makeover."

So I drew a big purple bow on the top of her head. Cora drew hoop earrings on her ears—or at

least where her ears would be, if spiders had ears. And Maya drew a red high heel on every one of her eight feet.

"Snookums, dahh-ling!" I said, in my best fancy-pants English accent. "You look ravishing!"

"Maaaah-velous!" said Maya.

"Enchaaaanting!" gushed Cora.

Pearl came in, and as usual, she wanted to join the fun.

"Snookey so pwetty!" she agreed. "I wove you, Snookey!"

Then she puckered up and kissed that big, hairy, high-heeled, googly-eyed spider with all her heart.

The Fix-It Friends

When Maya's mom came to pick her up, Maya gave me a hug. "That was so fun, I forgot to be scared."

Every week, Maya came over. Sometimes Ezra or Cora came, too. Maya kept jumping up the steps on the staircase list Ezra had made for her.

Pretty soon, Maya stopped wearing her kitty hat to recess every day. That was good because it gave her a chance to do really cool hairstyles with her superlong hair sometimes. One day, she had her hair in a big, swirly bun on the top of her head, like a ballerina.

"Wowza!" I said when I saw her. "You are a sight to behold!"

That's when I asked her if she took any special vitamins to make her hair grow so long, and she said, "Nope. None."

Figures. Some people have all the luck.

Have No Fear!

Jude found this book at the library for her that was full of up-close photographs of insects. Maya was really brave and forced herself to look at them, starting with the little ant and trying a bigger bug every time. Pearl really liked the book. Her favorite was the picture of the spider. Every time she saw it, she recited "Little Miss Muffet." Except she says it like this:

"Wittle Miss MuffMuff

Sat on her TuffTuff

Eatin' Kermit and waisins.

Awong came a 'pider

And sat down beside her

And he 'cared her. That naughty 'pider!"

She loved that rhyme so much, we decided for Halloween, I'd be Miss MuffMuff and she could be my spider. Maya laughed when I told her.

Chapter 13

A few days before Halloween, at recess, I was playing Vampire Tag with Cora and Camille and Noah and Minnie. When I stopped to drink water from the fountain, I saw that Maya wasn't sitting on her lunch box. She was standing up by the fence. She looked like she was really itching to play.

So I said, "Wanna play tag with us?"

"I don't know how," she said.

"Oh, it's as easy as falling off a log!" Granny in Texas always says that, and it cracks me up. I said it with Granny's accent, which makes the word *log* sound like "laaaawg," so Maya laughed.

Have No Fear!

Then Ezra and Jude ran over and said they'd play, too, so Maya said, "Sure."

Vampire Tag is where the person who's "It" has to be a vampire. If that person tags you, it's like you have been bitten, and you're a vampire, too. Then you can bite other people by tagging them. You have to talk in a Transylvanian accent and say, "I vant to suck your blood!" a lot, which makes it extra fun.

First, Noah was It. He's so fast that he turned us all into vampires in two minutes. Next, Maya was It. She was a natural! She bit me right off the bat.

"Vy? Vy have you bitten me?!" I howled, grabbing my neck and pretending to be in terrible pain.

"I didn't vant to!" she moaned, pretending to cry. "Forgive me, von't you?"

It was one of my all-time favorite tag games.

When the whistle blew, I gave Maya a quick hug, then grabbed my lunch box so I could dart over to the red doors. Except that on my way over there, I bumped into something. A big, heavy thing. A human being thing.

Miss Tibbs was staring down at me. She had a very strange expression on her face. The corners of her mouth were pointing up, and you could see her teeth in between her lips. It looked exactly like a smile. But no! It couldn't be! Miss Tibbs never smiles! Not even with Cora.

"I see Miss Tanaka played with you today," she said.

"Umm, yeah," I replied. I looked around her body to see all the kids lining up by the red doors.

"She looked happy," Miss Tibbs said.

"She likes tag," I said. I was kind of nervous because Miss Tibbs talks to me only when I am in trouble.

That strange smile on Miss Tibbs's face got bigger. It looked weird on her, but I couldn't say so.

"I'm proud of you, Miss Conti," she said.

She didn't move out of my way like I thought she would. She just waited like she wanted me to say something back.

So I blurted out, "I'm proud of you, too!"

Then I dashed off and made it to the red doors

just before they closed. I was the very last person to walk in, but I didn't even care. It made me feel kind of wonderful that I'd been the first person in the history of the world to make Miss Tibbs smile. That smile made me think maybe she wasn't so bad after all. She was probably still a witch, but maybe not a wicked one.

Chapter 14

The last step on Super Maya's staircase list was "Go see a spider in real life." Maya's mom found out that the zoo was having a whole spider exhibit, and she invited me and Jude and Cora and Ezra to go with Maya. Then afterward, she said, we could have a celebration at her house with a Japanese dessert called mochi ice cream. I'd never tasted it before, but I knew I would like it, because I never met an ice cream I didn't like.

We went to the zoo the day before Halloween, so Maya's mom said we could wear our costumes if we wanted. Nana had made my Little Miss

MuffMuff costume from scratch. She used to be a seamstress, so she can sew anything you want. For Miss MuffMuff, she'd made me an old-fashioned yellow dress with a white sash and a white bonnet.

Cora dressed up like Little Orphan Annie. She looked perfect with her red curly hair.

Jude and Ezra dressed up as zombie killer bees. I was worried Maya would be scared, but they looked so funny with their crazy face paint, she just laughed.

And Maya dressed up like—who else?—Super Maya! She wore a shiny black superhero suit with a giant red *M* on the chest and a beautiful flowing red cape.

Even though Pearl was too little to come with us, she insisted on putting on her spider costume. Nana had made a black fur suit, and Dad had made the legs out of cardboard covered with black

Have No Fear!

electrical tape. The problem was, her legs stuck out so much, they kept knocking stuff over when she walked. She knocked over two glasses of milk, one vase of flowers, a picture frame, and the sculpture Jude had made of a great horned owl, in just about two minutes. Dad said it was going to be a long Halloween.

When we got to the zoo, the room with the spiders was dark. To be honest, it kind of gave *me* the heebie-jeebies. I could tell Jude felt creeped out, too. Maya's eyes were round and big, but she gritted her teeth like she meant business.

Ezra and Cora ran right into the spider room and were oohing and aahing and stuff. The rest of us just stood in the doorway with Maya's mom, holding hands.

"Well, should we go in?" I asked Maya. I was secretly hoping she would say no.

She took a big gulp of air, and then she said in a whisper, "I can do it. I am brave," to herself. Then she nodded, and we walked in a few steps.

"This is far enough," she said.

"Totally," Jude said.

We could see the spiders crawling around behind the glass, but they were far away, so we didn't have to

see their faces. Maya was breathing really fast like a dog who's been running around. Her hand was kind of sweaty.

Then Cora came running over to tell us about her favorite spider. "It's called a red-kneed tarantula. It has stripes all over its legs, and it's one of the biggest kinds of tarantula in the world! It can be up to seven inches! And it's from Mexico."

Guess who will never be going to Mexico? Me! Oh, and probably not Maya, either.

Then Ezra ran over, cracking his knuckles. "I saw the coolest spider! It's called a Chilean rose hair tarantula, and it's from Chile and it's got little red hairs all over its body!"

Guess who will never be going to Chile, either?

"And it can flick the hairs off its belly if it's being attacked to distract its predator. And they make really good pets. I'm going to ask my mom if we can get one! I think Ziggy would love some company."

Maya squeezed my hand. I squeezed back.

"Isn't it time for ice cream?" I asked.

Maya's mom said it certainly was. She gave Maya the biggest hug I've ever seen, and she said, "I'm so proud of you."

Back at Maya's house, we ate the mochi ice

cream. It comes in a ball! And it was green! I'm not even kidding. The flavor was green tea. It was de-lish! I had seconds . . . and thirds.

When we were all done, Ezra took out his laptop and opened up the Super Maya chart. He made Super Maya jump up on the very last step, which said, "Go see a spider in real life." That put her on the top of the mountain. When she jumped on it, rainbows started to spread behind her in the sky, and lollipops popped up out of the grass, and little white kittens jumped up and down and said, "Meow! Hooray! Meow!"

We all danced around and said, "Meow! Hooray! Meow!" and we laughed our faces off.

"I'm still a little scared of spiders," Maya said shyly.

"I'm still a little scared of getting sucked down the bathtub drain," I admitted.

Then Mom came to pick us up, and we went home. Mom was feeling really happy and proud of us, so when Jude and I asked if Cora and Ezra could sleep over, she said sure.

Chapter 15

Dad always calls sleepovers "sleepless-overs" because we stay up really late and hardly get any sleep.

Jude slept in his bed on the top bunk, and Ezra slept in my bed on the bottom. Me and Cora made a big comfy floor-bed with tons of blankets and pillows and all my stuffed dogs.

Mom and Dad let us stay up late watching *Singin' in the Rain*, which was Ezra's pick. He always chooses old movies to watch, and I don't mind them as long as they are not black-and-white. Nothing is more boring than a movie with no colors in it.

As soon as the movie was over, Mom and Dad said it was Lights-Out. Of course, that doesn't mean you have to go to sleep; it just means you have to whisper.

I was thinking about Maya and how cool it was that she'd faced her fear and could enjoy the good things in life again, like recess.

"Hey, guys," I whispered, "thanks for helping me help Maya."

"No big deal," said Jude. "I actually kind of liked doing it."

"Totally," said Ezra.

"Me, too," squeaked Cora.

"Me, too," said a mysterious voice next to me. I pulled down the blanket and saw Pearl in her favorite pj's, with purple unicorns all over them. She calls them "uni-corn-on-the-cobs," which totally cracks us up. She was holding Ricardo and sucking on her pacifier.

"Pearly, what are you doing in here?" I asked her.

"Wanna sweep over!" Pearl said. She covered herself and Ricardo with my blanket.

"Okay, but *shhhhhh* or Mom and Dad will hear you!" I told her.

Everything was quiet for a minute, and then I whispered, "I feel kind of bummed that we're done helping Maya. Because it just feels so great. Like,

Maya was miserable and now she's not, and part of the reason is us!"

"Well, she's not the only kid in the world who has a problem," Jude said.

"What do you mean?" I asked.

"I mean, if it feels so great, you could always help someone else."

That is when I got my big idea. I had a "Eureka! moment," as Mom would say.

"GUYS!" I shouted. "I've GOT it!"

"*Shhhhhh!*" they all said, even Pearl.

I was so excited, I jumped up. "We should find someone else and help them!"

"That's exactly what I just said," Jude grumbled.

"We'll be a group of problem solvers! Friends that fix problems! We'll be the Fix-It Friends!" I shrieked.

Have No Fear!

Cora squeaked, "That would be wonderful."

And Ezra said, "Cool."

Jude tilted his head to the side and squinted his eyes like he was thinking reeeeeally hard about it. "Why not?" he said.

"Yippee-ki-yay!" I shouted. I was so excited, I did a cartwheel right there on the spot. It was almost a perfect cartwheel . . . until my foot knocked over the plastic tub of marbles on Jude's desk.

The sound of four billion marbles hitting the floor is even louder than the sound of four billion pennies hitting the floor.

"Oopsy daisy," I said.

"Oopsy daisy," giggled Pearl.

Dad came in, looking tired and grumpy. He told us to pick up all those marbles or we were going to eat rocks for breakfast. Then he said something about how this is exactly why he hates sleepless-overs. Then he took Pearl and put her back in her bedroom.

"Well, it didn't take long to find another problem to solve," giggled Cora as she scooped up marbles.

"Yeah, I have a feeling that Ronny will make sure we always have plenty of problems," Jude said.

I was going to clobber him, but I had to admit, it was pretty funny.

"The Fix-It Friends," I shouted, "to the rescue!"

Take the Fix-It Friends Pledge!

I, (say your full name), do solemnly vow to help kids with their problems. I promise to be kind with my words and actions. I will try to help very annoying brothers even though they probably won't ever need help because they're soooooo perfect. Cross my heart, hope to cry, eat a gross old garbage fly.

When Worry Weighs You Down . . .

Do you sometimes get really worried? Maybe you're scared of tarantulas . . . or tornadoes . . . or throw-up. Maybe you're scared, and you don't know why exactly. No matter what you worry about or how much you worry, one thing's for sure: You're not the only one! Tons of other kids feel exactly the same way.

What does worry feel like?

"I want to hide."
—Liam, age seven

"It feels like a weight you're carrying around."
—Harper, age eleven

"My heart pounds, and I just want to run away."
—Annie, age eight

"It feels like there's a gate in my brain, and whenever I'm afraid, that gate opens and all my fears run through and have a battle with my common sense."

—Giovanni, age ten

What helps?

"Taking deep breaths makes me feel better. I say, 'Roses in,' and inhale and then, 'Sharp thorns out,' and breathe out."

—Stella, age eight

"I hug my doll, Jessie. She takes care of everything for me—even bad dreams and thunder."

—Hannah, age eight

"I just remember that it will go away and that everybody has a little anxiety, even grown-ups."

—Frank, age nine

"You can't push worry away until you actually do what you're worried about. Then you feel like you accomplished something, and it feels good."

—Emma, age nine

What to Do When You Worry

Worry is like an alarm going off in your head. Sometimes, it's a real alarm that protects you from danger, like when it stops you from touching a steaming pot on the stove or petting a wild grizzly bear. But sometimes it's a false alarm, blaring really loudly even though you're perfectly safe. It doesn't protect you—in fact, it keeps you from doing cool stuff you really want to do, like playing at recess or swimming in a lake or talking to a new friend.

Good news! Even though you didn't turn the Worry Alarm on, you can turn it off. No, not all at once, but slowly and steadily. Here's how:

1. Tell a grown-up.

Sometimes just talking to someone about how you're feeling makes you feel better. Plus, a grown-up you trust can help you with these next steps!

2. Trash worry thoughts.

Worry sends your brain lots of scary messages that usually start with a what-if, like, *What if that spider is poisonous? What if everyone laughs at me? What if the bus is too bumpy and I get sick?* Whenever a what-if message gets delivered to your brain, picture yourself sticking a big neon label on it that says, WARNING! THIS MESSAGE IS FROM WORRY! DO NOT OPEN! Then toss that worry thought in the trash.

3. Talk back to your worry.

Use the facts and your super-smart

brain to correct Worry's messed-up thinking. If you're nervous about a poisonous spider, remind yourself, "Those are really rare. This spider's probably harmless. Anyway, it won't bother me if I just leave it alone." Worry can be a big bully, but you can talk back and show him who's the boss by telling yourself, "I'm brave! I can do this!"

4. Do stuff that scares you, a little at a time.

If you're scared of riding the bus, and you don't get on it, the next time you see that bus, it's going to seem scarier, and the time after that, it'll be even scarier. But if you get on the bus the first time, it will seem less and less terrifying. So it's really important to face your fear . . . but you don't have to do it all at once. You can take as long as you need and conquer your fear in little steps. For example, maybe you ride the bus for only one stop the first time. Do what works for you; just keep on being brave.

Remember, you're stronger than you think! You can *totally* kick Worry's booty. And when you do, you should treat yourself to your favorite ice cream . . . with a big ol' pile of whipped cream on top.

Want more tips or fixes for other problems? Just want to check out some Fix-It Friends games and activities? Go to fixitfriendsbooks.com!

Resources for Parents

If your child is struggling with anxiety, here are some resources that may be helpful.

Books for Kids

Is a Worry Worrying You? by Ferida Wolff and Harriet May Savitz, Tanglewood Press, 2005

Wemberly Worried by Kevin Henkes, Greenwillow Books, 2010

What to Do When You Worry Too Much: A Kid's Guide to Overcoming Anxiety by Dawn Huebner, Magination Press, 2006

Wilma Jean the Worry Machine by Julia Cook, National Center for Youth Issues, 2012

Books for Parents

Freeing Your Child from Anxiety: Powerful, Practical Solutions to Overcome Your Child's Fears, Worries, and

Phobias by Tamar Chansky, PhD, Harmony, 2004

Helping Your Anxious Child: A Step-by-Step Guide for Parents by Ronald Rapee, PhD; Ann Wignall, DPsych; Susan Spence, PhD; Heidi Lyneham, PhD; Vanessa Cobham, PhD, New Harbinger Publications, 2008

Websites

Worrywise

www.worrywisekids.org

NYU Child Study Center

www.aboutourkids.org

Anxiety and Depression Association of America

www.adaa.org

Coping Cat Parents

www.copingcatparents.com

FIND A COGNITIVE BEHAVIORAL THERAPIST:

Association for Behavioral and Cognitive Therapies

www.abctcentral.org

Don't miss the next adventure of

The Fix-It Friends

Sticks and Stones!

About the Author

Nicole C. Kear grew up in New York City, where she still lives with her husband, three firecracker kids, and a ridiculously fluffy hamster. She's written lots of essays and a memoir, *Now I See You*, for grown-ups, and she's thrilled to be writing for kids, who make her think hard and laugh harder. She has a bunch of fancy, boring diplomas and one red clown nose from circus school. Seriously.

nicolekear.com